D1440860

Loose Leaves in Tea

Jane Voneman DuPerow

LOOSE LEAVES IN TEA

Jane Voneman DuPerow

ISBN: 978-1-66786-708-3

CHAPTER 1

Jane is a psychic, a medium. She meditates daily, and eats a plant-based diet. She has very strong gifts of psychic and intuitive abilities. She had them even when she was growing up as a child but did not understand her gifts very well, so it scared her, and she had no support from her family. She was raised in a white-collar upper-class family, and she went to Catholic grade school, where the nuns were very mean to her. She was always afraid of things as a child, like she was worried that he would be possessed by demons later in life.

She was in a severe car accident where she lost her spleen, and then she had her near-death experience, where she saw an angel. This is what led her to the psychic sixth sense and inner knowing. She traveled to learn many things and took classes on how to train herself deeper into states of consciousness and succeeded, having a hugely successful business as a psychic and a medium. She does remote viewing, during which she is able to see a movie screen image in her head, a vision. If she asks her spirits a question, she gets the answer through the vision, and she is also clairaudient, which means that she can hear her spirits talking to her. She has intense visions that tell her things. She is able to hear what her friends think of her, or she can speak through a radio, a technique that only top psychics can do, where they can hear each other in their ear from far away. That is, even if one psychic is in New York and she wants to talk to him, she can just tune in the dial and can hear and see a vision. She's extremely gifted as a medium and sees dead people. She also was born in Salem, Massachusetts, right on Halloween, so her dad always called her his little witch growing up and would give her silver spoons that he collected on his travel for business She was conceived in a little town near Silver Creek, New York, which was right outside of a psychic community called Lilydale. She loved to do psychic readings daily and helped many people with her gifts. She even read for law enforcement in missing persons cases.

CHAPTER 2

Jane lived in a small Victorian cottage in Richmond, Virginia. Her house had southern charm with gingerbread and shutters that were pink. She had a grand chandelier in the dining room and many rugs from India and Tiffany lamps in every room of the house. She loved collecting teapots, and she had teas from all over the world. She had Victorian-style vintage furniture with goose-down pillows and fabrics from Peru. She had statues of Isis, Lakshmi, and Ganesha and many candles and tinctures for healing bruise, like nettles, mugwort, and wormwood, for her rituals of magic.

That morning she awoke to a feeling and divination of a great storm. She saw the swirling wind and cyclone form into a tornado. She leaped out of bed and made her tea. It was her favorite chamomile tea with almond milk. She gently felt Chloe at her leg rubbing against it and purring, and she went over to the cupboard to get tuna to feed the cat. Also, Jane smacked her lips as she drank her tea with honey "Yum this is good, Chloe." She wanted to have company that day even though the weather was looking uninviting. "A storm brewed," she said to her cat, which was a black Abyssinian cat, a breed originated from the temples of Egypt. Chloe nudged her leg lovingly and was hungry. Her black cat was a magical cat. It was her familiar, and every time the weather looked like it was going to be giving Jane a hard time, her cat would lie in one corner of the spare bedroom off to the side of the house. She had magical altars in every room, and altars for every direction, north, southeast, and west. The one in the south was for abundance of prosperity and success in Jane's business. Her psychic medium business proved popular by many, and she did at least three readings daily. She used to do eight readings a day and parties every weekend, but she lessened that because of psychic burnout and did fewer readings lately. She ran a mystery school of magic also, and people would come from all over the city to Richmond to meditate and learn more on how to be intuitive to tap more into their psychic abilities. She mostly focused on her clients, but tonight she was supposed to have the mystery school over at her house to meditate. Jane loved to entertain her guests, and always had great food, all vegan and raw that she made herself, like rolled up oat cookies with dates and coconut flakes and cinnamon and nut butter and coconut oil. She enjoyed cooking daily, and she always ate a plant-based diet. She had herbal infusions in every cup, and she made nettles infusions, ashwaganda, and cinnamon latte. She was always working on herself and her psychic gifts, but she had to really meditate a lot to focus in on cases for the missing or her clients before they showed up for a reading.

Jane knew the town called her the local witch. That they did this did not really bother her, but she did not try to broadcast that she was a witch after all. She did not know her own power. She knew that she could make street lamps turn off by themselves and many things happen if she wanted it to, but she never abused her power and only stayed in the light, She called it whitelighter magic, where she vowed only to help heal people like in the old days when there were midwives and healers with tinctures and remedies, the old witches who were misunderstood and burned at the stake, yes, and they were hugely misunderstood.

CHAPTER 3

She went down to her altar in the south and lit a candle and did her chanting this morning. Her altar in the south was to bring her good fortune and abundance of prosperity. It was a technique used by Feng shui. She started chanting her regular abundance chant, "om shree kamalova mahalakshmi Raja swaha." She learned this chant was for abundance, and she learned it from a very powerful witch in New York, named Rea.

She then did her normal routine and jumped on her trampoline for a while. It was in her kitchen, and it helped cleanse the body of toxins. She drank huge amounts of water, and she was always working on peak health. She also held her crystals regularly to recharge her body and was always getting drained from channeling many spirits for her regular clients. But the crystals would always help recharge her batteries. Sometimes she built crystal grids in her home and took photos of how beautiful they were. She burned her sage that morning also to help with spirits and to invoke them. She also used Palo de Santo Jain and trained with the best teachers out there. She met up with Jain, her mentor. He was a very powerful guru, and he taught Jane how to tap into her psychic abilities. She was already born with powerful gifts, but she worked hard on achieving them daily by meditation, proper diet, and tae kwon do. She once went in on a spiritual word retreat where she did ice baths daily and two hours of meditation blindfolded. It really helped her work through her blocks and open her psychic potential more. She continuously spoke through the radio to her teacher and mentor, Jain. She also did radio shows and even had a little television community cable access show of her own in her hometown.

Her grandmother was Marty Burfi and she used to read her tea leaves when Jane was just five years old. That is where she thinks she inherited some of her grandmother's psychic abilities. Jane moved about her house that day preparing to get out. She felt the weather forming in the vision. She realized that she had not swept up her cat, Chloe, under her arms and talked to her cat for a while.

She had an inner knowing that she was accurate on her tornado vision. Plus, Chloe was trying to get back upstairs to sit in that corner in the spare room again. She glanced outside and saw a green sky and heard the locomotives around that a tornado was in the mix. She grabbed her cat and ran into the tornado cellar.

Outside, the trees were swaying and branches were already starting to break. She heard an owl hoot very loudly outside, and she made a mad dash into the cellar. Her home was one hundred years old, built with tornado cellars already coming with the original plans of the home. Jane climbed down the ladder, with Chloe clawing her on the arm and holding on very tight to Jane. The door over the top of her head was very hard to close. The wind started to swirl and howl around the cellar door. She had had a tough time getting it shut, but she managed to shut the door above and lock it. Chloe started screaming and clawing, and Jane settled her down and put her on the ground near the dirt.

CHAPTER 4

It was dark now in the cellar, and she managed to fumble around and find the lantern that she left down there with the matches. She lit the candle inside the lantern. The tornado was now going over her head in the cellar. She was scared but managed to remain pretty calm, and then she looked over to her right and saw a dead girl and her spirit standing there. Jane was quite alarmed that she saw the little girl and her spirit, but she was used to seeing dead people. However, it was odd that during a tornado a spirit would come to her. "Hello, I'm Bella." The ghostly haunting girl was standing there with warning and message-like eyes staring right into Jane, as if it were giving her a strong message. Bella was dressed in shorts and a blouse and also held a lantern in her hand, or what Jane thought was her hand. He also appeared to be holding a crystal that was lit up. Bella's hair looked trampled and messy. Her one pigtail was undone, and the other side of her hair was just flapping in the wind that was coming in a crack from the top of the tornado cellar. Bella had deep eyes that were in pain and blackened as if someone gave her a black eye.

The door kept on making a bumping sound, but Bella started to speak to her. You need to save the others. Please hurry. There is not much time left. They will not be safe. Jane saw a vision of the girl's physical body in a river in the next town over, and then Jane saw a vision of the perpetrator who abducted the girl, Bella. His name was Charles. The spirit was stuck in a dimension until she got a message across to someone to seek justice. This was called and earthbound spread, which could not make it onto the light until someone solves the mystery of where and when their disappearance happened, so that the families can have closure and peace. Bella just happened to pick Jane the medium, who was very clear on what happened to Bella.

CHAPTER 5

Tan and leaves of silt green pools in a mossy blouse floating down a river, her body lay resting on a riverbank in the city, and the icy cool waters of the river in the next town over, Alexandria, Virginia. Alexandria was a very upper-class community but had a river that not many people went by. Another flash of the vision blows a blouse, floating down the river. The blouse was lying in the water as if the mud was stuck and the leaves all around it. Jane embraced the vision as she knew it was something very important about Bella's disappearance. The tornado was over and Jane was very shaken. With her cat, she climbed out of the cellar to see the damage done by the storm. She was not able to get inside her house very well, but managed. There were some shutters that blew off her home and tree branches lying over her garden that she had just planted. Even though all of this in the earth was shaking around her, Jane smelled a scent of roses in the air. The debris from the storm was very apparent, but she immediately ran into her house and called the local law enforcement that she had worked with in the past, so that she could speak to the detective and the children sex crime unit. Jane also went right to her computer and logged into the center for missing children cases website and saw Bella's photo there. Jane got those pins and needles again in her body that told her that something huge in her life was about to happen to her.

Jane got into her red Mustang and went down to the police station. In the road on the way, there were many branches, but the tornado had not been that bad really. She walked into the station and asked to speak to Tom Hardy, the regular detective who worked on the missing persons cases, but he was on vacation and there was a fill in for him. His name was Brad.

Brad spoke to Jane that day at the police station, and he wrote everything down that she had told him. She had to fill out the necessary paperwork to report a crime. It was already on record at the station in Richmond, Virginia, that she was an accurate psychic medium who had solved many a cold case. Brad was intrigued, but still a little skeptical. He had just gotten his promotion on the police force and started to work in the children's sex crime department.

Jane went home that evening back to her cat and was exhausted. She called her group that was supposed to come over for her mystery school and canceled it because of the storm. Everyone was scared to go out anyway.

Brad had told her that he was going to come over the next morning to follow up on the vision of the location of missing Bella. Jane leaped out of bed that morning nervous because she knew what she was about to encounter, and seeing it always affected her emotionally. Despite the uncomfortable twist in her stomach, Jane knew she had to lead the way for Bella to be found, but her anxiety was through the roof. She then went home, exhausted, and agreed to meet Brad the next morning to go find the body.

Brad arrived at nine that morning. He was standing on the front porch and looked at the damage of her house, that her shutters had blown off from the storm. Brad shook his head, what a tornado, he thought. He rang the bell, and Jane hurried up to open the door for him to come in. She had put on yellow clothing that day for illumination. She had bright red lipstick on with no makeup other than that. She was utterly beautiful and was a divine angel walking the earth to her clients. She helped so many lives. She gave peace and closure as if her psychic gifts were from God.

She opened the door and had another flash of a vision. She saw herself kissing Brad in an embrace, and she took a deep breath and shook off the vision and opened the door. There he stood, looking so handsome it seemed that time had slowed down for a moment while she stood there. Her jaw dropped open a little. Brad was also for a split second mesmerized by Jane's beauty although he tried to act as if nothing was affecting him. It caught him off guard because he had not felt that it that night before, but something seemed very familiar to Brad about Jane. What could it be? He wondered if he had seen her before.

He shook her hand, and she left Brad inside her house. He looked around and commented on the decorations that she had. He lifted up a box. It was gifted to Jane from her grandma. He looked at it and studied it for a second. He sat down on her couch slowly while holding the box and said to Jane that this is very nice woodcarving. Jane asked him to open it. It was a music box that her grandpa had made, and it was left to her from her family. Brad commented on how nice it was because he loved to carve wood himself and make things like this.

Brad made small talk for a while, but then he got straight to the missing girl and wanted to know every detail of the vision where she felt the body was located. She and Brad went to his car so that they could go fast to see where Jane thought she was. She got into his vehicle and noticed a small dream catcher in the rearview mirror. Brad had liked going to Native American gatherings and went to a couple in his lifetime. He was Native American, and his family's bloodline also only had a trace of it. He had attended a buffalo dance once and did a vision quest. He had an undercover law enforcement vehicle and Jane felt comfortable sitting in the energy field of Brad and his leather seats. He had brought her a cup of coffee since it was early in the morning and had it sitting in his vehicle. It was a little chilly on that morning, so Jane bundled up her sweater that she had brought with her and put it over her legs. She started a casual conversation with Brad on the way to Alexandria. She spoke to him about how they had Native American heritage in common. She had done vision questing in the woods where she saw three orbs come over the trees. While she was fasting on her vision quest, she told Brad about the experience, and he felt that it was very powerful. They instantly felt a chemistry with each other right off the bat. Jane was single after a long rough divorce, and so was Brad.

Jane felt that familiar feeling in her body when she is attracted to someone, and she felt his energy and his attraction to her back. Brad was driving, so he just enjoyed talking to Jane although he kept looking at her and seeing how beautiful and soft her skin looked, and her lips were so red with lipstick as she sipped her coffee.

CHAPTER 6

They arrived at the small dirt road Jane had told Brad to go to. She knew exactly where it was. She led the way for Brad through the one wooded area, and there by the river was little Bella's dead body lying there on the ground. Her blouse was floating in the mossy green of the river, and the leaves around it just like Jane's vision. Jane gasped to see the body of little Bella lifeless, but so pretty. A little girl, around eight years old, Jane felt so much grief well up in her, and she spoke to Bella. I am so sorry for this terrible injustice that happened to you little Bella. I will find him. I swear by oath for you that I will save other victims of this heinous crime. I am so very sorry he did this to you. Jane felt such an emotion of turmoil and pain well up inside of her body that she started to shake. She was experiencing everything all over again, flashes of visions of how he had hit little Bella over the head with a piece of wood from a tree trunk and flung her down after he had his way with little Bella. Jane felt every detail of this panic-stricken feeling that Bella had in her heart before she died a death of horror. The intense fear of Bella was brought on by choking and biting the perpetrator, trying to shake and flail her legs around to escape. But he had her down in a chokehold at first and held her arm down, and then he hit her over the head again and again as pure innocent blood trickled out onto the leaves. Jane felt the coldness of the blood on her hands and face while she was viewing everything that had happened. Jane was numb. She just sat there and started trembling and crying as Brad tried to remain calm. She actually wailed for poor little Bella because she was so pretty and such a fragile child.

Brad brought a cloth from the trunk of his car to put over the body and started to put police yellow tape around the trees. He called on the radio for other law enforcement to come and do the tracking of the DNA and all the evidence. He told Jane to walk away from Bella and sit in the car. Jane saw another vision of Bella and her spirit smiling at her as if Bella knew now she could go into the light to God. Jane saw bright light, which was almost blinding as it took Bella and her spirit up to the heavens.

The police came with the sniffing dogs to do the tracking of the footsteps of the perpetrator and get the scent. The forensic unit did the dusting and the looking at all the evidence under the nails of the girl. There was dirt as if she scratched the ground with her fingernails. The forensic team dusted and printed the area. Maybe the dirt under Bella's nails gave some clue into it.

Jane was totally exhausted at this point. It was so emotional for her. Brad took her back home as the other law enforcement people did the work they needed to do and brought Bella's body to the morgue for the parents to identify her.

Brad was afraid to approach the parents, but he had to go over to their home. He had already questioned the parents, and they had put up a reward for their daughter. Her name was Bella Palsley. The parents were in a severe state of shock when Brad went to the door. "We have found the body of your daughter and we want you to come down to the morgue and see if this is your daughter." The mother, Irene, almost passed out, but frantically she got in the car with Brad and her husband. Jane was at home resting from the whole ordeal and she fell asleep, and that night she had a dream.

Jane went the next morning with Brad to the morgue. As she walked through the big metal doors into the morgue, she walks slowly down the ice-cold hallway with the energy being very intense. She looked at Bella lying there dead in her physical form, and she saw another flash of a vision of other children standing over Bella in spirit claiming that they were also abducted and killed by the same perpetrator who had killed little Bella. She went home again, exhausted after her bad experience at the morgue.

CHAPTER 7

Jane's Dream

Jane's dream started out very slowly. She saw dancing lambs from childhood on the wooden white crib. The lambs were painted on the headboard of the crib when Jane was a baby. When her sister Jean was a little girl, she had stuck her finger in a light socket, and her sister saw the vision of the dancing lambs come alive on the grip. She got a shock and a little burn, but her sister was okay. Jane saw this memory in her dream and then saw her birth happening and that she was born with a tiny hole near her neck. The doctor had to skin graft over it. Jane was born in Salem, Massachusetts, and she feels that she was in a past life with Brad.

Jane awoke that morning and saw a memory of herself growing up as a child. She had gone to camp Christopher one year with her cousins Marsha and Mary Kay. That was the last time she was able to see them before they died in a terrible car accident, with her aunt Janet driving the station wagon that hit a tree. The girls were in the back, and their bodies flew through the windshield. Jane remembered that night very clearly. Her mom was on the phone getting the news of the accident as a spool of thread gathered and came unwound on her mother's body as she ran around the house hysterical crying. No, she would not tell Jane right away what happened. Her mom yelled "I can't tell you, Jane," and her sister started laughing then because of the spool of thread was wrapped around their mom. But later on the way to her cousins' house, they told her and recited the rosary, while Jane and Jean were in the back seat going to pick up Jane's brother Jim. Jane knew now what happened to her cousins. They were gone. Jane used to figure skate on the ice every year in the winter with Marsha and Mary Kay. She pondered their death, but she was very young at the time when it happened so she was confused as to what emotion to feel. But when she grew up as an adult, then she started really hurting over it. She would have dreams of the girls, Marsha and Mary Kay, all the time. She would have dreams that they were missing at sea, but Jane would find them on a boat. She would be was so happy that there they were alive again in her dreams. Spirits often came from other dimensions to crossover, astral travel, and meet in the dreamtime. The person who's dreaming meets them halfway in the other dimension like a visit from the other side.

Jane always wondered if her aunt Janet was mad at trees or life after the loss of her precious children. Jane thought of the great tree of life and how trees seemed to have a human face on them sometimes as if they take on a humanlike form their roots strongly rooted in the ground going down into the earth twisting and winding their greatness she thought of. The Mayans and many tribes used to go to the great tree of life to gain answers from it, like going to God. Jane often caught herself hugging trees and gathering the cheat energy from them.

Jane pondered more while lying in bed. She woke up stiff and achy after all the stress of all the visions and the power and the emotions of finding a young victim deceased. She was scared of her own power again how accurate she was as a psychic medium. She also started to feel butterflies in her stomach about the feeling that she may have for Brad and she prayed by her altar in the east that morning. And in the other spare room, her cat was purring and content.

CHAPTER 8

Jean

Jane sister Jean called her and asked her if she knew what a willow wisp was. Her sister wanted to know what it meant to her period. Jane thought of it as a sign from her sister. It was magical like that the connection she had with her sister. It was a spiritual message to Jane. A willow wisp is a fairy sprite who came in the form of a beam of light. Also a bit of fluorescent light and the willow wisp can lead you astray. That is what Jane thought about her path right now. As if she knew in her gut that she was going to be led astray by something soon, hopefully not Brad and an attraction. She told her sister everything she had gone through lately. Her sister was stunned on the phone with her. Jane made some tea.

Jane remembered the dancing lambs and the crib again that her sister reminded her of. Her sister Jean was in California on a trip. Jane was jealous because she wanted to travel, but right now it was time for work.

Jane was refreshed and rested after she spoke to her sister. She told her all about Brad and how she was attracted to him. Jean was shocked. She did not think Jane would ever get attracted to anyone again.

Jane was refreshed and rested again after she talked to her sister Jean. Brad called her and wanted to come over again, so Jane hung up the phone after saying goodbye to her sister, and clicked over to Brad on the other line and said okay. Brad came to her house, brought her another cup of coffee, and drove her again to the morgue. Jane went down the icy-cold building hallway after Brad open the heavy door for her to enter. She went to the body again of Bella on the table and closed her eyes. A flash came, and there were four little girls standing there. Jane yelled out to Brad, "We have to act fast before he kills other children." Jane was not sure if these children were alive in the vision or their spirits were already deceased.

CHAPTER 9

New Love

Brad brought her back home and told her to pack a suitcase. Jane knew it was all the way to West Virginia that they had to travel to find the perpetrator and the other missing children. They might have to stay overnight even in a hotel because it was a very long drive and they would both be worn out.

Jane and Brad were exhausted when they arrived in the state of West Virginia. She was very shook up, and anxiety was taking a hold of her. They got to the hotel, and there was only one room available. Jane wanted to get separate rooms, but she knew later that she had to remain cautious with Brad, but hopefully not to sleep too soundly later because she did not know Brad that well. Her worry started to manifest into feeling an attraction to Brad because she was going through so much intent emotions already. She felt like it was a coping mechanism to her pain and grief for having to witness Bella lying dead on the ground in the wooded area.

Jane went into the bathroom and put her pajamas on as Brad watched the news that evening. They had arrived in West Virginia that evening around 7:00 p.m. Brad was very good looking. He had chiseled features and blond hair. He was athletic and took great care of himself, but he was also very shook up about the missing girl and telling the parents because it was first time ever that he had to do that. Brad was really trying to cope with the whole thing also. While Jane was in the shower, she tried to meditate but kept getting feelings also of Brad outside the door. They were so mentally and physically drained and exhausted from the crime to poor little Bella that they had to mentally find a coping mechanism to take themselves out of getting too emotionally attached to the case.

Brad now studied Jane's backside as she walked into the bathroom and shut the door. He felt his manhood rising up, and he tried to put a pillow over it. But he was really feeling those endorphins rise up. His testosterone was getting all over the place, and the energy in the room shifted. Jane could feel it on the other end and looked in the mirror and said "no" to herself and "you are not going to give in to this feeling of temptation or emotion plus you do not even know him that well."

She walked out of the bathroom and saw Brad looking so amazing and shy as if he was a little boy again. She heard a cat out of the window meowing and she thought of her cat, Chloe, at home. "I cannot stay long tomorrow," she said nervously, and she sat down on the bed. "I have to get home quick tomorrow to feed my cat. I had no one to feed her for me." Brad, nervous, said, "Yeah, we will. We will just see what you feel tomorrow, and then I will drive you back, scout's honor," and he put his hand up like a Boy Scout would do. Jane looked at his boyish face and how he had a dimple on his chin. She smiled nervously at Brad's laugh, straightened out her energy, and felt a little bit better. Brad felt better too, and they laughed together for a while and sat and watched the news in quiet. All of a sudden on the news was the information of the missing child dead, Bella Palsley. Brad was upset because they were not supposed to leak it to the news stations yet and the media.

Brad tried to go to sleep that evening. He could not shut his eyes. Jane lay there also and that familiar feeling overcame her. She could feel that familiar feeling in her, and she tried to avoid this feeling as best she could, but she felt Brad awake lying in the bed next to her. Her mind went from attraction to Brad to horror of what just happened in their life, witnessing a crime. The light side of her took over, and she just lay there numb and stared at the wall. She could not sleep at all. Brad was going through the same thing. They felt the pull psychologically to each other to deal with things and cope.

Brad said to Jane, "Are you okay? Can you sleep at all? I am having some trouble getting to sleep. Do you want to talk?" At this point, she could not even speak. Brad was having lots of difficulty wanting to just take Jane and swoop her up in his arms and lie on the bed next to her and make mad passionate love to her that night. "Oh God," he said to himself. "What in the hell am I going to do," he whispered under his breath as to not let Jane hear him, but she knew too that he was struggling with the attraction. Knowing that this was so intense for both of them, he sat up. She sat up as well in the bed, and they looked at each other. Their eyes looked alike in desperation panic. They gave in. They just could not resist any longer. Brad walked over to Jane's bed and started kissing her. She mumbled,

"I can't." He respected it and stopped. She gave in, and passionately embraced him in the passionate long kiss. It felt so amazing. She allowed Brett to rip her pajamas off, and they made love that night. Jane felt such peace in her body and pleasure and rapture all wrapped up into one. Brad was a great love maker.

The next morning, they both stumbled to the coffee maker not quite awake. They smiled again at each other, and Brad said, "Well, we had better do this." Jane said, "About last night . . . Brad said, "Let's just keep it to ourselves and not worry right now about our future." Jane felt the same as if she could not handle the fact of falling in love right now, but they were falling in love with each other. That morning, Jane went to the bathroom and looked at herself in the mirror. Why did this happen? She felt zapped from the emotional havoc reaped on her body and also dealing with the vision of a crime scene horror. At the same time, she felt like it was going to cause all of her emotions to let go too soon. Brad thought about how beautiful she looked in the beam of sunlight that caught her body in the morning. She had wrapped a sheet over herself to cover herself and drank her coffee, but he also knew that serious business was to begin and he felt guilt as he managed to also get dressed and compose himself and come back to himself. They both needed to solve the crime and catch the perpetrator or the serial killer who was going around harming children. They were on a missing person's case to save children's lives, so why did they resort to breaking down and having intimacy with each other period. No one had the answer to that except for the great spirit.

Jane started thinking about the serial killer and was getting flashes of visions again of him. She told Brad that they had to hurry

LOOSE LEAVES IN TEA

and leave soon. They walked out of the hotel, and they got into the car and proceeded to the town in West Virginia that was their destination. She had the feeling that the perpetrator was a man named Charles.

CHAPTER 10

Charles

Charles was in a pool hall that morning already drinking beer. He had left the cabin that he was renting in the woods. It was all rundown. There, in the cabin, was another little girl, called Angel, who had been missing. That morning, her parents did not even know she was gone. She had stood at the bus stop and Charles had lured her in with a puppy dog that he told her he was going to bring to her home that morning to give her mom. He asked Angel if she knew where the house was so he could deliver the puppy. Angel, all happy, said, "Sure, I will show you where my mom lives. It's right over there." She climbed in the car with him and the puppy dog, and he brought Angel to the cabin. She was very scared. He put a sock in her mouth and laid her on a bed and put duct tape over her mouth. She was in a state of shock and fell fast asleep.

Charles came back from the pool hall, picked up Angel, and walked out into the other room with a fireplace and lit a fire. He thought about what he was going to do with Angel. He was a sick pedophile who had already done time in jail for other crimes, mainly theft, but always had a sick attraction to young girls and child pornography. He also always watched movies that he would get online of children being forced to have sex with adults. He was an evil, sick monster who had a very hard life growing up as a child and was also beaten and sexually molested by his father daily.

Charles could not help his sex addiction and his sick behavior, and he had never found any help for it but through drugs and alcohol. It made him feel worse once he tried to have a relationship with a woman. He beat her until she was almost dead, and she never pressed charges or spoke to him again. The rumor in town was that everyone knew not to mess with him because he was very strange, but no one in town really knew how sick he was.

Jane saw the next vision: it was Charles at the McGuffey Pool Hall. Brad asked, "Are you sure this is where you feel the perp hangs out, Jane?" She said, "Yes, I'm very sure of it." He drove her to the pool hall, which was very seedy-looking bar that was very rundown. Brad got out of the car and told Jane to stay inside the car.

Brad went inside and saw Charles with all of his tattoos and fitting the description that Jane had told him that the perpetrator would look like. Brad walked over and asked Charles if he ever met a girl named Bella Palsley and showed him a photo. Charles of, course, said no. And with a cigarette hanging out of his mouth, he looked Brad up and down, said, "Ooh, you're nice," and went to grab him right in the crotch. Brad got out the handcuffs and said, "You are under arrest for killing Bella Palsey." Charles yelled and kicked and screamed and said he did not do it. Charles somehow managed to kick Brad really hard in the head, and ran out the door. He saw Jane was there, and she looked Charles in the eyes. He ran away. Jane was so alarmed she ran into the bar and saw Brad lying there with blood gushing from his head. She helped him to return to life and get the blood off by patting his head with a rag that the bartender gave her. At this point, Jane had another vision. There was a cabin in the vision, and the girl, Angel, lying on the bed with duct tape and a sock in her mouth asleep. Then Brad started to become coherent again. He asked Jane if she saw him, and she said yes. Then she saw Charles running out of the bar and heading toward some woods.

Jane saw another vision of Charles getting ready to run back to the victim. She got another vision of an address that she could barely make out in her mind's eye, but thought she had got the vision accurately of where the cabin was located. She told Brad to go down that road. Brad radioed in to the law enforcement that he needed assistance to come and help, but Charles ran and escaped. Charles made it back to the cabin, and he was out of breath from running so fast. It was nestled in the woods around twenty-five minutes running distance from the seedy bar in the town of Roanoke, West Virginia.

He had the little girl inside. She was going to be his next victim. She was alive but sedated as she gave into the chloroform. She had started to awaken, and her eyes were blindfolded and she had duct tape over her mouth. She started to try to move and shake in the bed and scream, but he did not go help her at all. Jane and Brad drove around for hours trying to remain calm, and she needed to focus on what and where this cabin was in the woods. It was difficult to find, and they were getting lost a lot. She started freaking out and panicking that he was going to kill the next little girl if they did not get there fast.

There was hardly any time remaining. She told Brad to hurry up or they would both be sorry. Brad drove over creeks of water not caring at all about his undercover cop vehicle. They went up and down, and Jane hit her head on the top of the roof of the car inside. While he was trying to speed up to 65 mph on a dirt road, Jane sensed they were close. There was a sort of ravine over the river, and there she saw the cabin at the top of the hill. They had to climb out of the car to make it up the hill to the cabin.

They got to the cabin and looked inside the window where they saw Charles sitting on a withered couch smoking a cigarette. They went around to the next window and saw Angel lying there on the bed blindfolded, hands tied. Brad drew his gun out slowly while he told Jane to go back away from the cabin because he did not want her to get hurt. He was sweaty and had blood all over his shirt. Charles heard the leaves rustle outside and darted out the front door of the cabin, running again through the woods to try to escape Brad, but Brad managed this time to shoot Charles in the leg. He fell to the ground in pain. Brad had handcuffed Charles to a tree and left him there while Brad and Jane managed to get into the cabin and see the little girl lying there. She was just starting to awaken and she yelled, "Mommy."

Jane and Brad spoke to the little girl and told her that everything would be okay. The rest of the police were called to the cabin, and they took Charles away to the city jail to hold him until his court date. He was prosecuted for first-degree murder. He was a cold calculating man and deserved the death sentence if the judge decided to give it to him, seeing that he was a serial killer of children.

CHAPTER 11

The Good Starts to Happen to Jane

Jane deserved a medal for what she had done, but it was all volunteer work and no one really knew of what she did because she kept it to herself. She felt so fulfilled and had an inner reward of saving child victims of sex crimes. She felt in her heart that she helped the world and humanity.

Now Jane could finally get back to her life as a psychic medium helping her clients daily. She went back home, but she never forgot Brad. He had dropped her back, hugged her goodbye, and told her to keep in touch. She did keep in touch by seeing visions of him daily on the job in the morning getting his coffee. He decided to get up the nerve to finally call her and ask her how she was doing. She was so happy to hear from him, and he invited himself over to her house and sat smiling at each other on her sofa in her home. Jane saw another vision that she and Brad were to be married later that summer, and a child was on the way. It was her first child. Jane had become pregnant after that night of passion in West Virginia. Jane knew it right from the moment of conception, but she waited until she did a pregnancy test and confirmed it to herself.

Jane and Brad were married later that year after only five months of knowing each other. Jane's mystery school was over, and Bradley moved in with her. Jane was pregnant with their child. Jane could take a year off since Brad made enough money to support and raise their child. They had a gorgeous baby girl, the kind that Jane wanted her whole life. They lived happily ever after in Jane's Victorian home with her cat, Chloe, and now the child. Brad spoiled Jane every morning, getting chamomile tea for her and helping her to keep the house tidy and letting in her clients on his days off from work. Jane and Brad lived happily ever after.

THE END